# THOMAS & FRIENDS

# THOMAS
## Gets His Own Branch Line

Illustrated by
Tommy Stubbs

## Random House 🏠 New York
Thomas the Tank Engine & Friends

**A BRITT ALLCROFT COMPANY PRODUCTION**
Based on The Railway Series by the Rev W Awdry. Copyright © Gullane (Thomas) LLC 2002.

www.randomhouse.com/kids    www.thomasthetankengine.com

*Library of Congress Cataloging-in-Publication Data*
Thomas gets his own branch line / illustrated by Tommy Stubbs. — 1st ed.  p.  cm.
"Based on the Railway series by the Rev. W. Awdry."
SUMMARY: Before Thomas can become a Really Useful Engine, he has to learn a great deal
about responsibility, patience, and cooperation.
ISBN 0-375-82213-5
[1. Railroads—Trains—Fiction.]  I. Stubbs, Tommy, ill.  II. Awdry, W. Railway series.
PZ7.T3694973· 2002  [E]—dc21  2002005576

Printed in the United States of America   First Edition   10 9 8 7 6 5 4 3 2 1

When Thomas first came to the Big Station, he was a cheeky little engine with no experience and not very many good manners. He liked to play tricks on the other engines. And sometimes he would rush to finish a job quickly and make a careless mistake. He thought that no engine worked as hard as he did.

Thomas had a lot to learn before he could become a Really Useful Engine.

One day, Thomas was shunting coaches in the yard. But he didn't think pushing coaches around was a very important job. He decided to play a trick on Gordon instead.

When Gordon came chugging into the yard,
Thomas steamed out from behind a tree and overturned a
truck full of cement right onto Gordon's wheels.

Gordon was stuck! "Now I cannot pull the
Express!" he grumbled.

Thomas just laughed and laughed.
*"Peep, peep! Peep!"*

But the joke did not seem *quite* so funny when Sir Topham Hatt came marching up with an angry look on his face.

"Thomas, where are the coaches?" he demanded. "People all over Sodor will be upset if the Express is late! Everyone expects this railway to be Really Reliable and Right on Time." Then Sir Topham Hatt hurried off to see if Henry could pull the Express.

"I'm sorry, Gordon," said Thomas. "I thought my trick would be funny." And he quickly went to get the coaches that he was supposed to have lined up earlier.

As he raced off, Thomas could hear Gordon still grumbling. "Cheeky little engine . . ."

Thomas worked quickly to get all the coaches. "Hurry, hurry," he pleaded. "The Express is going to be late!"

Thomas shunted all the coaches into place just as Henry was ready to go.

The Express was off, just in the nick of time!

When all the commotion was over and Gordon was unstuck and cleaned, Thomas got a good talking-to.

Sir Topham Hatt said, "Really Useful Engines do *not* play tricks when they have work to do! Shunting coaches may not seem important, but it is. If the coaches are not lined up properly, the passengers cannot ride the railway.

"*But* I am pleased that you worked hard to correct your mistake and get the Express going on time. Really Useful Engines take their duties seriously, and you have learned that every job is important."

After that, Thomas worked very hard. He played only *after* his work was done. But he wished that he could pull coaches filled with passengers instead of just pushing empty coaches around the yard.

One morning, Thomas' wish was granted. Henry was too sick to pull his morning route, and Thomas was the only engine left in the station.

"You'll have to pull Henry's train, Thomas," said Sir Topham Hatt. "We are counting on you. And *no* tricks!"

"Yes, sir!" Thomas hurried away. He just *knew* he could do as good a job as any of the big engines.

Thomas puffed eagerly into the station where the coaches and the passengers were waiting.

"Calm down, Thomas," said his driver. "Really Useful Engines are patient and careful with their work."

But Thomas didn't pay him any mind. He quickly backed up to the coaches.

Then, without waiting for the "all clear" signal, he chugged out of the station.

Thomas puffed along the line. He was very proud of himself. When he reached a "stop" signal, he slowed down in a huff. *Why should a speedy train like me have to wait for a pesky signal?* he thought. *"Peep, peep!"* he whistled impatiently.

The signalman came running out. "Hello, Thomas. What are you doing out of the yard?" he asked.

"Can't you see? I'm pulling Henry's coaches," peeped Thomas.

"I don't see any coaches," said the signalman.

Thomas' driver looked over his shoulder. There *were* no coaches. Thomas had left them behind at the station!

Thomas was so disappointed that he almost cried.
"Don't worry, Thomas," said his driver. "We'll go back and get the coaches straightaway."

Thomas went back and got the coaches. He waited until the coaches were properly hitched. Soon they were back on schedule. At each station, Thomas was very careful to let all the passengers on and off. "Thank you, Thomas," they said.

When Thomas got back to the yard that night, he was very tired. Pulling coaches was harder than he had thought. Sir Topham Hatt was waiting for him, trying not to smile.

"You did just fine, Thomas, once you remembered to get the coaches. . . ." Sir Topham Hatt chuckled. "More important, you learned something: Really Useful Engines are patient as well as speedy."

The next week, Thomas was pulling the afternoon train. When he came to the first station, he noticed an engine that wasn't on the track. "Hello, I'm Thomas," he said. "Why aren't you on the track?"

"Pleased to meet you, Thomas. I'm Bertie. I'm not on the track because I'm not a train. I'm a bus. Buses take passengers just like trains, but we drive on roads instead of on tracks," Bertie said.

"Well, a *bus* can't be as fast as a *train*," said Thomas cheekily. "I bet I can get to the end of the line before you." And he raced off.

Thomas was trying so hard to beat Bertie that he forgot to stop at the stations to let the passengers off! They started to get angry.

Thomas' driver shouted, "Stop, Thomas, stop!"

But Thomas was going so fast that he could only hear the wind whistling.

Thomas got to the end of the line. "I won!" he peeped. "I *knew* trains were faster than buses."

"But, Thomas," the driver said angrily, "you haven't let any of your passengers off."

"Oh, no," gasped Thomas. "How will I get all these people home before dark?"

Just then, Bertie came driving up. "I'll help you," said Bertie.

"You will help me?" Thomas asked. "Even though I was very cheeky?!?"

"Of course," said Bertie. "We all help each other on the Island of Sodor."

And Thomas and Bertie split up the passengers and took them all home.

Once again, Thomas got a talking-to from Sir Topham Hatt. "Thomas, today you made two mistakes: one when you raced against Bertie and another when you forgot to let off your passengers. But in the end, you and Bertie got all the passengers safely home. I hope you have learned that although trains and buses are different, it does not mean that one is better than the other. *And* things work out when you work together."

Thomas *was* learning new lessons
every day, and he really liked his new
responsibilities. One day, he was pushing some
Troublesome Trucks in the yard when he saw
James going by much too fast.

"Help, help!" James called. "The trucks are pushing me too fast. And my brakes are on fire!"

The Troublesome Trucks only laughed and called, "On, on! Faster! Faster!"

Thomas acted quickly. He hitched himself to the breakdown train and hurried down the line after James.

When Thomas found James, he had run right off the line and was lying in a muddy ditch.

Thomas helped to get James and all the trucks back onto the track.

"Thank you, Thomas," said James. "You knew *just* what to do."

When Thomas and James got back to the yard, Sir Topham Hatt was waiting for them. "Thomas, I am very proud of you. You were brave, cool-headed, and helpful. You have grown quite a bit from the cheeky little engine you used to be. You have proven that you truly are a Really Useful Engine. Because you have done such a good job, I have decided that you shall have your own branch line!"

Thomas couldn't believe it. He was so excited. *"Peep, peep, peeeeeeeep!!"* he cried happily as he raced around the yard.